○全民阅读·经典小丛书○

新月集

[印]泰戈尔⊙著
冯慧娟⊙编

吉林出版集团股份有限公司

版权所有　侵权必究

图书在版编目（CIP）数据

新月集 /（印）泰戈尔著；冯慧娟编. —长春：吉林出版集团股份有限公司，2015.6（2025.5重印）
（全民阅读. 经典小丛书）
ISBN 978-7-5534-7795-4

Ⅰ.①新… Ⅱ.①泰…②冯… Ⅲ.①诗集–印度–现代 Ⅳ.①I351.25

中国版本图书馆 CIP 数据核字 (2015) 第 128460 号

XIN YUE JI
新月集

[印] 泰戈尔　著　　冯慧娟　编

出版策划：	崔文辉
选题策划：	冯子龙
责任编辑：	姜婷婷
排　　版：	新华智品
出　　版：	吉林出版集团股份有限公司
	（长春市福祉大路 5788 号，邮政编码：130118）
发　　行：	吉林出版集团译文图书经营有限公司
	（http://shop34896900.taobao.com）
电　　话：	总编办 0431-81629909　　营销部 0431-81629880 / 81629881
印　　刷：	北京一鑫印务有限责任公司
开　　本：	640mm × 940mm 1/16
印　　张：	10
字　　数：	130 千字
版　　次：	2015 年 10 月第 1 版
印　　次：	2025 年 5 月第 5 次印刷
书　　号：	ISBN 978-7-5534-7795-4
定　　价：	45.00 元

印装错误请与承印厂联系　　电话：010-61424266

前言

泰戈尔（Rabindranath Tagore，1861~1941年），印度诗人、小说家、戏剧家和社会活动家。他是第一个获得诺贝尔文学奖的亚洲人。泰戈尔一生创作颇丰，尤以诗歌最多，其代表作有《吉檀迦利》《飞鸟集》《新月集》《园丁集》《采果集》等。其作品思想深刻，内容博大精深，奠定了印度近代文学的基础，也为东方文学赢得了世界声誉。

泰戈尔是一位伟大的诗人，更是一位胸怀宽广的哲人，郑振铎曾说："泰戈尔的歌声虽有时沉寂，但是只要有人类在世上，他的微妙、幽宛之诗，仍将永远是自人类的心中唱出来的。"

《新月集》是泰戈尔从自己的孟加拉语诗中选摘翻译为英文的。在《新月集》中，泰戈尔延续了他一贯的诗风，以一颗赤子之心阐述了他对自然、宇宙和人生的哲理思索。《新月集》通过对儿童们的游戏的描写，巧妙地表现了儿童的心理及丰富的想象力，为我们展示了一个纯洁美好的儿童世界。那一首首诗仿佛具有深不可测的魔力，将我们从复杂的成人世界带回简单快乐的童年时期，让我们重新忆起儿时的美好。同时，他的诗像珍珠一样闪耀着深邃的哲理光芒，也唤起了我们对一切美好事物的爱心，深深启迪着我们。

　　经典无国界。为了方便读者阅读，我们将《新月集》以中英文对照的形式辑录在一起，其中的英文部分系泰戈尔自译，中文为中国文学家郑振铎亲译。一流的水平加上大师的引导，一定能带给您语言和文学的双重魅力。

Contents

目录

THE HOME 家庭	8
BABY'S WAY 孩童之道	11
THE UNHEEDED PAGEANT 不被注意的花饰	16
SLEEP-STEALER 偷睡眠者	21
THE BEGINNING 开始	27
BABY'S WORLD 孩子的世界	31
DEFAMATION 责备	34
THE JUDGE 审判官	38
PLAYTHINGS 玩具	40
THE ASTRONOMER 天文家	43
CLOUDS AND WAVES 云与波	47
THE CHAMPA FLOWER 金色花	52
FAIRYLAND 仙人世界	56
THE LAND OF THE EXILE 流放的地方	61
THE RAINY DAY 雨天	67
PAPER BOATS 纸船	71

THE SAILOR 水手 ……………	74
THE FURTHER BANK 对岸 …………	78
THE FLOWER-SCHOOL 花的学校 ……	83
THE MERCHANT 商人 ……………	87
SYMPATHY 同情 ………………	92
VOCATION 职业 ………………	94
SUPERIOR 长者 ………………	99
THE LITTLE BIG MAN 小大人 ………	103
TWELVE O'CLOCK 十二点钟 ………	108
AUTHORSHIP 著作家 ……………	110
THE WICKED POSTMAN 恶邮差 ……	115
THE HERO 英雄 ………………	120
THE END 告别 ………………	128
THE RECALL 召唤 ……………	132
THE FIRST JASMINES 第一次的茉莉 …	135
THE BANYAN TREE 榕树 …………	139
BENEDICTION 祝福 ……………	142
THE GIFT 赠品 ………………	145
MY SONG 我的歌 ……………	148
THE CHILD-ANGEL 孩子天使 ………	151
THE LAST BARGAIN 最后的买卖 ……	154

THE HOME

家庭

I paced alone on the road across the field while the sunset was hiding its last gold like a miser.

我独自在横跨过田地的路上走着,夕阳像一个守财奴似的,正藏起它的最后的金子。

The daylight sank deeper and deeper into the darkness, and the widowed land, whose harvest had been reaped, lay silent.

白昼更加深沉地投入黑暗之中,那已经收割了的孤寂的田地,默默地躺在那里。

Suddenly a boy's shrill voice rose into the sky. He traversed the dark unseen, leaving the track of his song across the hush of the evening.

天空里突然升起了一个男孩子的尖锐的歌声。他穿过看不见的黑暗,留下他的歌声的辙痕,跨过黄昏的静谧。

His village home lay there at the end of the waste land, beyond the sugar-cane field, hidden among the shadows of the banana and the slender areca palm, the cocoa-nut and the dark green jack-fruit trees.

他的乡村的家坐落在荒凉的土地的边上，在甘蔗田的后面，躲藏在香蕉树、瘦长的槟榔树、椰子树和深绿色的波罗蜜树的阴影里。

I stopped for a moment in my lonely way under the starlight, and saw spread before me the darkened earth surrounding with her arms countless homes furnished with cradles and beds, mothers'hearts and evening lamps, and young lives glad with a gladness that knows nothing of its value for the world.

我在星光下独自走着的路上停留了一会儿,看见黑沉沉的大地展开在我的面前,用她的手臂拥抱着无数的家庭。在那些家庭里有着摇篮和床铺,母亲们的心和夜晚的灯,还有年轻的生命,他们满心欢乐,却浑然不知这样的欢乐对于世界的价值。

BABY'S WAY
孩童之道

If baby only wanted to, he could fly up to heaven this moment.

只要孩子愿意,他此刻便可飞上天去。

It is not for nothing that he does not leave us.

他所以不离开我们,并不是没有缘故。

He loves to rest his head on mother's bosom, and cannot ever bear to lose sight of her.

他爱把他的头倚在妈妈的胸间,他即使是一刻不见她,也是不行的。

Baby knows all manner of wise words, though few on earth can understand their meaning.

孩子知道各式各样的聪明话,虽然世间的人很少懂得这些话的意义。

It is not for nothing that he never wants to speak.

他所以永不想说,并不是没有缘故。

The one thing he wants is to learn mother's words from mother's lips. That is why he looks so innocent.

他所要做的一件事,就是要学习从妈妈的嘴唇里说出来的话。那就是他所以看来这样天真的缘故。

Baby had a heap of gold and pearls, yet he came like a beggar on to this earth.

孩子有成堆的黄金与珠子，但他到这个世界上来，却像一个乞丐。

It is not for nothing he came in such a disguise.
他所以这样乔装打扮了来，并不是没有缘故。

This dear little naked mendicant pretends to be utterly helpless, so that he may beg for mother's wealth of love.
这个可爱的小小的裸着身体的乞丐，所以假装着完全无助的样子，便是想要乞求妈妈的爱的财富。

Baby was so free from every tie in the land of the tiny crescent moon.
孩子在纤小的新月的世界里，是一切束缚都没有的。

It was not for nothing he gave up his freedom.
他所以放弃了他的自由，并不是没有缘故。

He knows that there is room for endless joy in mother's little corner of a heart, and it is sweeter far than liberty to be

The Crescent Moon

caught and pressed in her dear arms.

他知道有无穷的快乐藏在妈妈的心的小小一隅里，被妈妈亲爱的手臂拥抱，其甜美远胜过自由。

Baby never knew how to cry. He dwelt in the land of perfect bliss.

孩子永不知道如何哭泣。他所住的是完全的乐土。

It is not for nothing he has chosen to shed tears.

他所以要流泪,并不是没有缘故。

Though with the smile of his dear face he draws mother's yearning heart to him, yet his little cries over tiny troubles weave the double bond of pity and love.

虽然他用了可爱的脸儿上的微笑,引逗得他妈妈的热切的心向着他,然而他的因为细故而发的小小的哭声,却编成了怜与爱的双重约束的带子。

THE UNHEEDED PAGEANT

不被注意的花饰

Ah, who was it coloured that little frock, my child, and covered your sweet limbs with that little red tunic?

呵，谁给那件小外衫染上颜色的，我的孩子？谁使你的温软的肢体穿上那件红的小外衫的？

You have come out in the morning to play in the courtyard, tottering and tumbling as you run.

你在早晨就跑到院子里玩儿，你，跑着就像摇摇欲跌似的。

But who was it coloured that little frock, my child?

但是谁给那件小外衫染上颜色的，我的孩子？

What is it makes you laugh, my little life-bud?

什么事叫你大笑起来的，我的小小的命芽儿？

Mother smiles at you standing on the threshold.

妈妈站在门边,微笑着望着你。

She claps her hands and her bracelets jingle, and you dance with your bamboo stick in your hand like a tiny little shepherd.

她拍着双手,她的手镯叮当地响着;你手里拿着你的竹竿儿在跳舞,活像一个小小的牧羊人。

But what is it makes you laugh, my little life-bud?

但是什么事叫你大笑起来的,我的小小的命芽儿?

O beggar, what do you beg for, clinging to your mother's neck with both your hands?

喔,乞丐,你双手攀搂住妈妈的头颈,要乞讨些什么?

O greedy heart, shall I pluck the world like a fruit from the sky to place it on your little rosy palm?

喔,贪得无厌的心,要我把整个世界从天上摘下来，像摘一个果子似的，把它放在你的一双小小的玫瑰色的手掌上么？

O beggar, what are you begging for?

喔，乞丐，你要乞讨些什么？

The wind carries away in glee the tinkling of your anklet bells.

风高兴地带走了你踝铃的叮当。

The sun smiles and watches your toilet.

太阳微笑着,望着你的打扮。

The sky watches over you when you sleep in your mother's arms, and the morning comes tiptoe to your bed and kisses your eyes.

当你睡在妈妈的臂弯里时,天空在上面望着你,而早晨蹑手蹑脚地走到你的床跟前,吻着你的双眼。

The fairy mistress of dreams is coming towards you, flying through the twilight sky.

仙乡里的梦婆飞过朦胧的天空，向你飞来。

The world-mother keeps her seat by you in your mother's heart.

在你妈妈的心头上，那世界母亲，正和你坐在一块儿。

He who plays his music to the stars is standing at your window with his flute.

他，向星星奏乐的人，正拿着他的横笛，站在你的窗边。

SLEEP-STEALER

偷睡眠者

Who stole sleep from baby's eyes? I must know.

谁从孩子的眼里把睡眠偷了去呢？我一定要知道。

Clasping her pitcher to her waist mother went to fetch water from the village near by.

妈妈把她的水罐挟在腰间，走到近村汲水去了。

It was noon. The children's playtime was over; the ducks in the pond were silent.

这是正午的时候，孩子们游戏的时间已经过去了；池中的鸭子沉默无声。

The shepherd boy lay asleep under the shadow of the banyan tree.

牧童躺在榕树的树荫下睡着了。

The crane stood grave and still in the swamp near the mango grove.

白鹤庄重而安静地立在杧果树边的沼泽里。

In the meanwhile the sleep-stealer came and, snatching sleep from baby's eyes, flew away.

就在这个时候，偷睡眠者跑来从孩子的两眼里捉住睡眠,便飞去了。

When mother came back she found baby travelling the room over on all fours.

当妈妈回来时,她看见孩子四肢着地地在屋里爬着。

Who stole sleep from our baby's eyes? I must know. I must find her and chain her up.

谁从孩子的眼里把睡眠偷了去呢?我一定要知道。我一定要找到她,把她锁起来。

I must look into that dark cave, where, through boulders and scowling stones, trickles a tiny stream.

我一定要向那个黑洞里张望,在这个洞里,有一道小泉从圆的和有皱纹的石上滴下来。

I must search in the drowsy shade of the bakula grove, where pigeons coo in their corner, and fairies'anklets tinkle in the stillness of starry nights.

我一定要到醉花①林中的沉寂的树影里搜寻，在这林中，鸽子在它们住的地方咕咕地叫着，仙女的脚环在繁星满天的静夜里叮当地响着。

In the evening I will peep into the whispering silence of the bamboo forest, where fireflies squander their light, and will ask every creature I meet, "Can anybody tell me where the sleep-stealer lives?"

我要在黄昏时，向静静的萧萧的竹林里窥望，在这林中，萤火虫闪闪地耗费它们的光明，只要遇见一个人，我便要问他："谁能告诉我偷睡眠者住在什么地方？"

Who stole sleep from baby's eyes? I must know.

谁从孩子的眼里把睡眠偷了去呢？我一定要知道。

Shouldn't I give her a good lesson if I could only catch her!

只要我能捉住她，怕不会给她一顿好教训！

I would raid her nest and see where she hoards all her stolen sleep.

我要闯入她的巢穴，看她把所有偷来的睡眠藏在什么地方。

I would plunder it all, and carry it home.

我要把它们都夺来，带回家去。

I would bind her two wings securely, set her on the bank of the river, and then let her play at fishing with a reed among the rushes and water-lilies.

我要把她的双翼缚得紧紧的，把她放在河边，然后叫她拿一根芦苇在灯芯草和睡莲间钓鱼为戏。

When the marketing is over in the evening, and the village children sit in their mothers'laps, then the night birds will mockingly din her ears with:

黄昏，街上已经收了市，村里的孩子们都坐在

妈妈的膝上时,夜鸟便会讥笑地在她耳边说:

"Whose sleep will you steal now?"

"你现在还想偷谁的睡眠呢?"

【注释】

①醉花——印度传说:美女口中吐出香液,此花始开。

THE BEGINNING

开始

"Where have I come from, where did you pick me up?" the baby asked its mother.

"我是从哪儿来的,你,在哪儿把我捡起来的?"孩子问他的妈妈说。

She answered half crying, half laughing, and clasping the baby to her breast——"You were hidden in my heart as its desire, my darling.

她把孩子紧紧地搂在胸前,半哭半笑地答道——"你曾被我当作心愿藏在我的心里,我的宝贝。

"You were in the dolls of my childhood's games; and when with clay I made the image of my god every morning, I made and unmade you then.

"你曾存在于我孩童时代玩的泥娃娃身上;每天早晨我用泥土塑造我的神像,那时我反复地塑了又捏碎了的就是你。

"You were enshrined with our household deity, in his worship I worshipped you.

"你曾和我们的家庭守护神一同受到祀奉,我崇拜家神时也就崇拜了你。

"In all my hopes and my loves, in my life, in the life of my mother you have lived.

"你曾活在我所有的希望和爱情里,活在我的生命里,我母亲的生命里。

"In the lap of the deathless spirit who rules our home you have been nursed for ages.

"在主宰着我们家庭的不死的精灵的膝上,你已经被抚育了好多代了。

"When in girlhood my heart was opening its petals, you hovered as a fragrance about it.

"当我做女孩子的时候,我的心的花瓣儿张开,你就像一股花香似的散发出来。

"Your tender softness bloomed in my youthful limbs, like a glow in the sky before the sunrise.

"你的软软的温柔,在我的青春的肢体上开花了,像太阳出来之前的天空上的一片曙光。

"Heaven's first darling, twin-born with the morning light, you have floated down the stream of the world's life, and at last you have stranded on my heart.

"上天的第一宠儿,晨曦的孪生兄弟,你从世界

The Crescent Moon

的生命的溪流浮泛而下，终于停泊在我的心头。

"As I gaze on your face, mystery overwhelms me; you who belong to all have become mine.

"当我凝视你的脸蛋儿的时候，神秘之感淹没了我；你这属于一切人的，竟成了我的。

"For fear of losing you I hold you tight to my breast. What magic has snared the world's treasure in these slender arms of mine?"

"为了怕失掉你，我把你紧紧地搂在胸前。是什么魔术把这世界的宝贝引到我这双纤小的手臂里来呢？"

BABY'S WORLD
孩子的世界

I wish I could take a quiet corner in the heart of my baby's very own world.

我愿我能在我孩子自己的世界的中心，占一角清净地。

I know it has stars that talk to him, and a sky that stoops down to his face to amuse him with its silly clouds and rainbows.

我知道有星星同他说话，天空也在他面前垂下，用它傻傻的云朵和彩虹来娱悦他。

Those who make believe to be dumb, and look as if they never could move, come creeping to his window with their stories and with trays crowded with bright toys.

那些大家以为他是哑的人，那些看去像是永不会走动的人，都带了他们的故事，捧了满装着五颜六色的玩具的盘子，匍匐地来到他的窗前。

I wish I could travel by the road that crosses baby's mind, and out beyond all bounds;

我愿我能在横过孩子心中的道路上游行，解脱了一切的束缚；

Where messengers run errands for no cause between the kingdoms of kings of no history;

在那儿，使者奉了无所谓的使命奔走于无史的诸王的王国间；

Where reason makes kites of her laws and flies them, and truth sets fact free from its fetters.

在那儿,理智以她的法律造为纸鸢而飞放,真理也使事实从桎梏中自由了。

DEFAMATION

责备

Why are those tears in your eyes, my child?

为什么你眼里有了眼泪,我的孩子?

How horrid of them to be always scolding you for nothing?

他们真是可怕,常常无谓地责备你!

You have stained your fingers and face with ink while writing — is that why they call you dirty?

你写字时墨水玷污了你的手和脸——这就是他们所以骂你龌龊的缘故?

O, fie! Would they dare to call the full moon dirty because it has smudged its face with ink?

呵,呸!他们也敢因为圆圆的月儿用墨水涂了脸,便骂它龌龊么?

For every little trifle they blame you, my child. They are ready to find fault for nothing.

他们总要为了每一件小事去责备你,我的孩子。他们总是无谓地寻人错处。

You tore your clothes while playing—is that why they call you untidy?

你游戏时扯破了你的衣服——这就是他们所以说你不整洁的缘故么?

The Crescent Moon

O, fie! What would they call an autumn morning that smiles through its ragged clouds?

呵，呸！秋之晨从它的破碎的云衣中露出微笑。那么，他们要叫它什么呢？

Take no heed of what they say to you, my child.

他们对你说什么话，尽管可以不去理睬，我的孩子。

Take no heed of what they say to you, my child.

他们对你说什么话，尽管可以不去理睬，我的孩子。

They make a long list of your misdeeds. Everybody knows how you love sweet things—is that why they call you greedy?

他们把你做错的事长长地记了一笔账。谁都知道你是十分喜欢糖果的——这就是他们所以称你贪婪的缘故吗？

O, fie! What then would they call us who love you?

呵，呸！我们是喜欢你的，那么，他们要叫我们什么呢？

THE JUDGE

审判官

Say of him what you please, but I know my child's failings.

你想说他什么尽管说罢,但是我知道我孩子的短处。

I do not love him because he is good, but because he is my little child.

我爱他并不因为他好,只是因为他是我的小小的孩子。

How should you know how dear he can be when you try to weigh his merits against his faults?

你如果把他的好处与坏处两两相权一下,恐怕你就会知道他是如何的可爱罢?

When I must punish him he becomes all the more a part of my being.

当我必须责罚他的时候,他更成为我的生命的一部分了。

When I cause his tears to come my heart weeps with him.
当我使他眼泪流出时,我的心也和他同哭了。

I alone have a right to blame and punish, for he only may chastise who loves.
只有我才有权去骂他,去责罚他,因为只有热爱人的才可以惩戒人。

PLAYTHINGS

玩具

Child, how happy you are sitting in the dust, playing with a broken twig all the morning.

孩子,你真是快活呀,一早晨坐在泥土里,耍着折下来的小树枝儿。

I smile at your play with that little bit of a broken twig.

我微笑着看你在那里耍着那根折下来的小树枝儿。

I am busy with my accounts, adding up figures by the hour.

我正忙着算账,一小时一小时在那里加叠数字。

Perhaps you glance at me and think, "What a stupid game to spoil your morning with!"

也许你在看我,想道:"这种好没趣的游戏,竟把你的一早晨的好时间浪费掉了!"

Child, I have forgotten the art of being absorbed in sticks and mud-pies.

孩子，我忘了聚精会神地玩耍树枝与泥饼的方法了。

I seek out costly playthings, and gather lumps of gold and silver.

我寻求贵重的玩具，收集金块与银块。

The Crescent Moon

With whatever you find you create your glad games, I spend both my time and my strength over things I never can obtain.

你呢，无论找到什么便去做你的快乐的游戏，我呢，却把我的时间与力气都浪费在那些我永不能得到的东西上。

In my frail canoe I struggle to cross the sea of desire, and forget that I too am playing a game.

我在我的脆薄的独木船里挣扎着要航过欲望之海，竟忘了我也是在那里做游戏了。

THE ASTRONOMER

天文家

I only said, "When in the evening the round full moon gets entangled among the branches of that Kadam tree, couldn't somebody catch it?"

我不过说："当傍晚圆圆的满月挂在迦昙波①的枝头时，有人能去捉住它么？"

But dada [elder brother] laughed at me and said, "Baby, you are the silliest child I have ever known. The moon is ever so far from us, how could anybody catch it?"

哥哥却对我笑道："孩子呀，你真是我所见到的顶顶傻的孩子。月亮离我们这样远，谁能去捉住它呢？"

I said, "Dada, how foolish you are!When mother looks out of her window and smiles down at us playing, would you call her far away?"

我说："哥哥，你真傻！当妈妈向窗外探望，微笑着往下看我们游戏时,你也能说她远么?"

Still dada said, "You are a stupid child! But, baby, where could you find a net big enough to catch the moon with?"

哥哥还是说:"你这个傻孩子!但是,孩子,你到哪里去找一个大得能逮住月亮的网呢?"

I said, "Surely you could catch it with your hands."

我说:"你自然可以用双手去捉住它呀。"

But dada laughed and said, "You are the silliest child I have known. If it came nearer, you would see how big the moon is. "

但是哥哥还是笑着说:"你真是我所见到的顶顶傻的孩子!如果月亮走近了,你便知道它是多么大了。"

I said, "Dada, what nonsense they teach at your school! When mother bends her face down to kiss us does her face look very big?"

我说:"哥哥,你们学校里所教的,真是没有用呀!当妈妈低下脸儿跟我们亲嘴时,她的脸看来也是

The Crescent Moon

很大的么?"

But still dada says, "You are a stupid child."

但是哥哥还是说:"你真是一个傻孩子。"

【注释】

①迦昙波,原名Kadam,亦作Kadamba,学名Namlea Cadamba,意译"白花",即昙花。

CLOUDS AND WAVES

云与波

Mother, the folk who live up in the clouds call out to me—

妈妈,住在云端的人对我唤道——

"We play from the time we wake till the day ends.

"我们从醒的时候游戏到白日终止。

"We play with the golden dawn, we play with the silver moon."

"我们与黄金色的曙光游戏,我们与银白色的月亮游戏。"

I ask, "But, how am I to get up to you?"

我问道:"但是,我怎么能够上你那里去呢?"

They answer, "Come to the edge of the earth, lift up your hands to the sky, and you will be taken up into the clouds."

他们答道:"你到地球的边上来,举手向天,就可以被接到云端里来了。"

"My mother is waiting for me at home," I say. "How can I leave her and come?"

"我妈妈在家里等我呢,"我说,"我怎么能离开她而来呢?"

Then they smile and float away.

于是他们微笑着浮游而去。

But I know a nicer game than that, mother.

但是我知道一件比这个更好的游戏,妈妈。

I shall be the cloud and you the moon.

我做云,你做月亮。

I shall cover you with both my hands, and our house-top will be the blue sky.

我用两只手遮盖你,我们的屋顶就是青碧的天空。

The folk who live in the waves call out to me—

"We sing from morning till night; on and on we travel and know not where we pass."

住在波浪上的人对我唤道——

"我们从早晨唱歌到晚上;我们前进又前进地旅行,也不知我们所经过的是什么地方。"

I ask, "But, how am I to join you?"

我问道:"但是,我怎么能加入你们队伍里去呢?"

They tell me, "Come to the edge of the shore and stand with your eyes tight shut, and you will be carried out upon the waves."

他们告诉我说:"来到岸旁,站在那里,紧闭你的两眼,你就被带到波浪上来了。"

I say, "My mother always wants me at home in the evening — how can I leave her and go?"

我说:"傍晚的时候,我妈妈常要我在家里——我怎么能离开她而去呢!"

Then they smile, dance and pass by.
于是他们微笑着,跳舞着奔流过去。

But I know a better game than that.
但是我知道一件比这个更好的游戏。

I will be the waves and you will be a strange shore.

我是波浪,你是陌生的岸。

I shall roll on and on and on, and break upon your lap with laughter.

我奔流而进,进,进,笑哈哈地撞碎在你的膝上。

And no one in the world will know where we both are.

世界上就没有一个人会知道我们俩在什么地方。

THE CHAMPA FLOWER

金色花

Supposing I became a champa flower, just for fun, and grew on a branch high up that tree, and shook in the wind with laughter and danced upon the newly budded leaves, would you know me, mother?

假如我变了一朵金色花①,只是为了好玩,长在那棵树的高枝上,笑哈哈地在风中摇摆,又在新生的树叶上跳舞,妈妈,你会认识我么?

You would call, "Baby, where are you?" and I should laugh to myself and keep quite quiet.

你要是叫道:"孩子,你在哪里呀?"我暗暗地在那里匿笑,却一声儿不响。

I should slyly open my petals and watch you at your work.

我要悄悄地开放花瓣儿,看着你工作。

When after your bath, with wet hair spread on your shoulders, you walked through the shadow of the champa tree to the little court where you say your prayers, you would notice the scent of the flower, but not know that it came from me.

当你沐浴后，湿发披在两肩，穿过金色花的林荫，走到你做祷告的小庭院时，你会嗅到这花的香气，却不知道这香气是从我身上来的。

When after the midday meal you sat at the window reading Ramayana, and the tree's shadow fell over your hair and your lap, I should fling my wee little shadow on to the

The Crescent Moon

page of your book, just where you were reading.

当你吃过中饭,坐在窗前读《罗摩衍那》②,那棵树的阴影落在你的头发与膝上时,我便要投我的小小的影子在你的书页上,正投在你所读的地方。

But would you guess that it was the tiny shadow of your little child?

但是你会猜得出这就是你的小孩子的小小影子么?

When in the evening you went to the cowshed with the lighted lamp in your hand, I should suddenly drop on to the earth again and be your own baby once more, and beg you to tell me a story.

当你黄昏时拿了灯到牛棚里去,我便要突然地再落到地上来,又成了你的孩子,求你讲个故事给我听。

"Where have you been, you naughty child?"

"你到哪里去了,你这坏孩子?"

"I won't tell you, mother." That's what you and I would say then.

"我不告诉你，妈妈。"这就是你同我那时所要说的话了。

【注释】

①金色花，原名 Champa，亦作 Champak，学名 Michelia champacak，印度圣树，木兰科含笑属植物，开金黄色碎花。译名亦作"瞻波伽"或"占博伽"。

②《罗摩衍那》（Ramayana）为印度叙事诗，相传系蚁垤（Valmiki）所作。今传本形式约为公元二世纪间所形成。全书分为七卷，共二万四千颂，皆系叙述罗摩生平之作。罗摩即罗摩犍陀罗，十车王之子，悉多之夫。他于第二世（Tretayaga）入世，为毗湿奴神第七化身。印人视他为英雄，对他崇拜有加。

FAIRYLAND
仙人世界

If people came to know where my king's palace is, it would vanish into the air.

如果人们知道了我的国王的宫殿在哪里，它就会消失在空气中的。

The walls are of white silver and the roof of shining gold.

墙壁是白色的银，屋顶是耀眼的黄金。

The queen lives in a palace with seven courtyards, and she wears a jewel that cost all the wealth of seven kingdoms.

皇后住在有七个庭院的宫苑里；她戴的一串珠宝，值得整整七个王国的全部财富。

But let me tell you, mother, in a whisper, where my king's palace is.

不过，让我悄悄地告诉你，妈妈，我的国王的宫殿究竟在哪里。

It is at the corner of our terrace where the pot of the tulsi plant stands.

它就在我们阳台的角上，在那儿栽着杜尔茜花的花盆放着的地方。

The princess lies sleeping on the far away shore of the seven impassable seas.

公主躺在远远的隔着七个不可逾越的重洋的那一岸沉睡着。

There is none in the world who can find her but myself.

除了我自己，世界上便没有人能够找到她。

She has bracelets on her arms and pearl drops in her ears; her hair sweeps down upon the floor.

她臂上有镯子，耳上挂着珍珠；她的头发拖到地板上。

She will wake when I touch her with my magic wand,

and jewels will fall from her lips when she smiles.

当我用我的魔杖点触她的时候,她就会醒过来,而当她微笑时,珠玉将会从她唇边落下来。

But let me whisper in your ear, mother; she is there in the corner of our terrace where the pot of the tulsi plant stands.

不过,让我在我的耳朵边悄悄地告诉你,妈

妈,她就住在我们阳台的角上,在那栽着杜尔茜花的花盆放着的地方。

When it is time for you to go to the river for your bath, step up to that terrace on the roof.

当你要到河里洗澡的时候,你走上屋顶的那座阳台来罢。

I sit in the corner where the shadows of the walls meet together.

我就坐在墙的阴影所聚会的一个角落里。

Only puss is allowed to come with me, for she knows where the barber in the story lives.

我只让小猫儿跟我在一起,因为它知道那故事里的理发匠住的地方。

But let me whisper, mother, in your ear where the barber in the story lives.

不过，让我在你的耳朵边悄悄地告诉你，那故事里的理发匠到底住在哪里。

It is at the corner of the terrace where the pot of the tulsi plant stands.

他住的地方，就在阳台的角上，在那栽着杜尔茜花的花盆放着的地方。

THE LAND OF THE EXILE
流放的地方

Mother, the light has grown grey in the sky; I do not know what the time is.

妈妈．天空上的光成了灰色了；我不知道是什么时候了。

There is no fun in my play, so I have come to you. It is saturday, our holiday.

我玩得怪没劲儿的，所以到你这里来了。这是星期六，是我们的休息日。

Leave off your work, mother; sit here by the window and tell me where the desert of Tepantar in the fairy tale is?

放下你的活计，妈妈；坐在靠窗的一边，告诉我童话里的特潘塔沙漠在什么地方？

The shadow of the rains has covered the day from end

to end.

雨的影子遮掩了整个白天。

The fierce lightning is scratching the sky with its nails.

凶猛的电光用它的爪子抓着天空。

When the clouds rumble and it thunders, I love to be afraid in my heart and cling to you.

当乌云在轰轰地响着，天打着雷的时候，我总爱心里带着恐惧爬伏到你的身上。

When the heavy rain patters for hours on the bamboo leaves, and our windows shake and rattle at the gusts of wind, I like to sit alone in the room, mother, with you, and hear you talk about the desert of Tepantar in the fairy tale.

当大雨倾泻在竹叶子上好几个钟头，而我们的窗户被狂风震得格格发响的时候，我就爱独自和你坐在屋里,妈妈,听你讲童话里的特潘塔沙漠的故事。

Where is it. mother, on the shore of what sea, at the foot of what hills, in the kingdom of what king?

它在哪里,妈妈,在哪一个海洋的岸上,在哪些个山峰的脚下,在哪一个国王的国土里?

There are no hedges there to mark the fields, no footpath across it by which the villagers reach their village in the evening, or the woman who gathers dry sticks in the forest can bring herload to the market. With patches of yellow grass in the sand and only one tree where the pair of wise old birds have their nest, lies the desert of Tepantar.

田地上没有此疆彼壤的界石,也没有村人在黄昏时走回家的，或妇人在树林里捡拾枯枝而捆载到市场上去的道路。沙地上只有一小块一小块的黄色草地，只有一株树。就是那一对聪明的老鸟儿在那里做窝的．那个地方就是特潘塔沙漠。

I can imagine how, on just such a cloudy day, the young son of the king is riding alone on a grey horse through the desert, in search of the princess who lies imprisoned in the giant's palace across that unknown water.

我能够想象得到，就在这样一个乌云密布的日子，国王的年轻的儿子，怎样地独自骑着一匹灰色马，走过这个沙漠，去寻找那被囚禁在不可知的重洋之外的巨人宫里的公主。

When the haze of the rain comes down in the distant sky, and lightning starts up like a sudden fit of pain, does he remember his unhappy mother, abandoned by the king, sweeping the cow-stall and wiping her eyes, while he rides through the desert of Tepantar in the fairy tale?

当雨雾在遥远的天空下降,电光像一阵突然发作的痛楚的痉挛似的闪射的时候.他可记得他的不幸的母亲,为国王所弃,正在扫除牛棚,眼里流着眼泪,当他骑马走过童话里的特潘塔沙漠的时候?

See, mother, it is almost dark before the day is over, and there are no travellers yonder on the village road.

看,妈妈,一天还没有完,天色就差不多黑了,那边村庄的路上没有什么旅客了。

The shepherd boy has gone home early from the pasture, and men have left their fields to sit on mats under the eaves of their huts, watching the scowling clouds.

牧童早就从牧场上回家了,人们都已从田地里回来,坐在他们草屋的檐下的草席上,眼望着阴沉的云块。

Mother. I have left all my books on the shelf—do not ask me to do my lessons now.

妈妈,我把我所有的书本都放在书架上了——不要叫我现在做功课。

When I grow up and am big like my father, I shall learn all that must be learnt.

当我长大了,大得像爸爸一样的时候,我将会学到必须学的东西的。

But just for today, tell me, mother, where the desert of Tepantar in the fairy tale is?

但是,今天你可得告诉我,妈妈,童话里的特潘塔沙漠在什么地方?

THE RAINY DAY

雨天

Sullen clouds are gathering fast over the black fringe of the forest.

乌云很快地集拢在森林的黝黑的边缘上。

O child, do not go out!

孩子,不要出去呀!

The palm trees in a row by the lake are smiting their heads against the dismal sky; the crows with their draggled wings are silent on the tamarind branches, and the eastern bank of the river is haunted by a deepening gloom.

湖边的一行棕树,向暝暗的天空撞着头;羽毛零乱的乌鸦,静悄悄地栖在罗望子的枝上,河的东岸正被乌沉沉的暝色侵袭。

Our cow is lowing loud, tied at the fence.

我们的牛系在篱上,高声鸣叫。

O child, wait here till I bring her into the stall.

孩子,在这里等着,等我先把牛牵进牛棚里去。

Men have crowded into the flooded field to catch the fishes as they escape from the overflowing ponds; the rain water is running in rills through the narrow lanes like a laughing boy who has run away from his mother to tease her.

许多人都挤在池水泛溢的田间,捉那从泛溢的池中逃出来的鱼儿,雨水成了小河,流过狭街,好像一个嬉笑的孩子从他妈妈那里跑开,故意要恼她一样。

Listen, someone is shouting for the boatman at the ford.

听呀，有人在浅滩上喊船夫呢。

O child, the daylight is dim, and the crossing at the ferry is closed.

孩子，天色暝暗了，渡头的摆渡船已经停了。

The sky seems to ride fast upon the madly-rushing rain; the water in the river is loud and impatient; women have hastened home early from the Ganges with their filled pitchers.

天空好像是在滂沱的雨上快跑着；河里的水喧叫而且暴躁；妇人们早已拿着汲满了水的水罐，从恒河畔匆匆地回家了。

The evening lamps must be made ready.

夜里用的灯，一定要预备好。

O child, do not go out!

孩子，不要出去呀！

The Crescent Moon

The road to the market is desolate, the lane to the river is slippery. The wind is roaring and struggling among the bamboo branches like a wild beast tangled in a net.

到市场去的大道已没有人走，到河边去的小路又很滑。风在竹林里咆哮着，挣扎着，好像一只落在网中的野兽。

PAPER BOATS

纸船

Day by day I float my paper boats one by one down the running stream.

我每天把纸船一个个放在急流的溪中。

In big black letters I write my name on them and the name of the village where I live.

我用大黑字写我的名字和我住的村名在纸船上。

I hope that someone in some strange land will find them and know who I am.

我希望住在异地的人会得到这纸船，知道我是谁。

I load my little boats with shiuli flowers from our garden, and hope that these blooms of the dawn will be carried safely to land in the night.

我把园中长的秀利花载在我的小船上，希望这些黎明开的花能在夜里被平平安安地带到岸上。

I launch my paper boats and look up into the sky and see the little clouds setting their white bulging sails.

我投我的纸船到水里，仰望天空，看见小朵的云正张着满鼓着风的白帆。

I know not what playmate of mine in the sky sends them down the air to race with my boats!

我不知道天上有我的什么游伴把这些船放下来同我的船比赛！

When night comes I bury my face in my arms and dream that my paper boats float on and on under the midnight stars.

夜来了，我的脸埋在手臂里，梦见我的纸船在子夜的星光下缓缓地浮泛前去。

The fairies of sleep are sailing in them, and the lading is their baskets full of dreams.

睡仙坐在船里,带着满载着梦的篮子。

The Crescent Moon

THE SAILOR

水手

The boat of the boatman Madhu is moored at the wharf of Rajgunj.

船夫曼特胡的船只停泊在拉琪根琪码头。

It is uselessly laden with jute, and has been lying there idle forever so long.

这只船无用地装载着黄麻，无所事事地停泊在那里已经好久了。

If he would only lend me his boat, I should man her with a hundred oars, and hoist sails, five or six or seven.

只要他肯把他的船借给我，我就给它安装一百只桨，扬起五个或六个或七个布帆来。

I should never steer her to stupid markets.

我决不把它驾驶到愚蠢的市场上去。

I should sail the seven seas and the thirteen rivers of fairyland.

我将航行遍仙人世界里的七个大海和十三条河道。

But, mother, you won't weep for me in a corner.

但是,妈妈,你不要躲在角落里为我哭泣。

I am not going into the forest like Ramachandra to come back only after fourteen years.

我不会像罗摩犍陀罗①似的,到森林中去,一去十四年才回来。

I shall become the prince of the story, and fill my boat with whatever I like.

我将成为故事中的王子,把我的船装满了我所喜欢的东西。

I shall take my friend Ashu with me. We shall sail

merrily across the seven seas and the thirteen rivers of fairyland.

我将带我的朋友阿细和我作伴，我们要快快乐乐地航行于仙人世界里的七个大海和十三条河道。

We shall set sail in the early morning light.

我将在绝早的晨光里张帆航行。

When at noontide you are bathing at the pond, we shall be in the land of a strange king.

中午，你正在池塘里洗澡的时候，我们将在一个陌生的国王的国土上了。

We shall pass the ford of Tirpurni, and leave behind us the desert of Tepantar.

我们将经过特浦尼浅滩，把特潘塔沙漠抛落在我们的后边。

When we come back it will be getting dark, and I shall

tell you of all that we have seen.

当我们回来的时候,天色快黑了,我将告诉你我们所见到的一切。

I shall cross the seven seas and the thirteen rivers of fairyland.

我将越过仙人世界里的七个大海和十三条河道。

【注释】

①罗摩犍陀罗,即罗摩。他是印度叙事诗《罗摩衍那》中的主角。为了尊重父亲的诺言和维持弟兄间的友爱,他抛弃了继承王位的权利,和妻子悉多在森林中被放逐了十四年。

THE FURTHER BANK

对岸

I long to go over there to the further bank of the river。
我渴望到河的对岸去。

Where those boats are tied to the bamboo poles in a line;
在那边,好些船只一行儿系在竹竿上;

Where men cross over in their boats in the morning with ploughs on their shoulders to till their far away fields;
人们在早晨乘船渡过那边去,肩上扛着犁头,去耕耘他们的远处的田;

Where the cowherds make their lowing cattle swim across to the riverside pasture;
在那边,牧人使他们鸣叫着的牛游泳到河旁的牧场去;

Whence they all come back home in the evening, leaving the jackals to howl in the island overgrown with weeds.

黄昏的时候,他们都回家了,只留下豺狼在这满长着野草的岛上哀叫。

Mother, if you don't mind, I should like to become the boatman of the ferry when I am grown up.

妈妈,如果你不在意,我长大的时候,要做这渡船的船夫。

They say there are strange pools hidden behind that high bank.

据说有好些古怪的池塘藏在这个高岸之后。

Where flocks of wild ducks come when the rains are over, and thick reeds grow round the margins where waterbirds lay their eggs;

雨过去了，一群一群的野鹜飞到那里去，茂盛的芦苇在岸边四围生长，水鸟在那里生蛋；

Where snipes with their dancing tails stamp their tiny footprints upon the clean soft mud;

竹鸡带着跳舞的尾巴，将它们细小的足印印在洁净的软泥上；

Where in the evening the tall grasses crested with white flowers invite the moonbeam to float upon their waves.

黄昏的时候，长草顶着白花，邀月光在长草的波浪上浮游。

Mother, if you don't mind, I should like to become the boatman of the ferryboat when I am grown up.

妈妈，如果你不在意，我长大的时候，要做这渡船的船夫。

I shall cross and cross back from bank to bank, and all the boys and girls of the village will wonder at me while they are bathing.

我要自此岸至彼岸，渡过来，渡过去，所有村中正在那儿沐浴的男孩女孩，都要诧异地望着我。

When the sun climbs the mid sky and morning wears on to noon, I shall come running to you, saying, "Mother, I am hungry!"

太阳升到中天，早晨变为正午了，我将跑到你那里去，说道："妈妈，我饿了！"

When the day is done and the shadows cower under the trees, I shall come back in the dusk.

一天完了，影子俯伏在树底下，我便要在黄昏中回家来。

I shall never go away from you into the town to work like father.

我将永不同爸爸那样，离开你到城里去做事。

Mother, if you don't mind, I should like to become the boatman of the ferryboat when I am grown up.

妈妈，如果你不在意，我长大的时候，要做这渡船的船夫。

THE FLOWER-SCHOOL
花的学校

When storm clouds rumble in the sky and June showers come down,

当雷云在天上轰响，六月的阵雨落下的时候，

The moist east wind comes marching over the heath to blow its bagpipes among the bamboos.

润湿的东风走过荒野，在竹林中吹着口笛。

Then crowds of flowers come out of a sudden, from nobody knows where, and dance upon the grass in wild glee.

于是一群一群的花从无人知道的地方突然跑出来，在绿草上狂欢地跳着舞。

Mother, I really think the flowers go to school underground.

妈妈，我真的觉得那群花朵是在地下的学校里上学。

They do their lessons with doors shut, and if they want to come out to play before it is time, their master makes them stand in a corner.

他们关了门做功课,如果他们想在散学以前出来游戏,他们的老师是要罚他们站壁角的。

When the rains come they have their holidays.

雨一来,他们便放假了。

Branches clash together in the forest, and the leaves rustle in the wild wind, the thunder-clouds clap their giant hands and the flower children rush out in dresses of pink and yellow and white.

树枝在林中互相碰触着,绿叶在狂风里萧萧地响着,雷云拍着大手,花孩子们便在那时候穿了紫的、黄的、白的衣裳,冲了出来。

Do you know, mother, their home is in the sky, where

the stars are.

你可知道，妈妈，他们的家是在天上，在星星所住的地方。

Haven't you seen how eager they are to get there?
Don't you know why they are in such a hurry?

你没有看见他们怎样急着要到那儿去么？你不

The Crescent Moon

知道他们为什么那样急急忙忙么?

Of course, I can guess to whom they raise their arms: they have their mother as I have my own.

我自然能够猜得出他们是对谁扬起双臂来:他们也有他们的妈妈,就像我有我自己的妈妈一样。

THE MERCHANT
商人

Imagine, mother, that you are to stay at home and I am to travel into strange lands.

妈妈,让我们想象,你待在家里,我到异邦去旅行。

Imagine that my boat is ready at the landing fully laden.

再想象,我的船已经装得满满的在码头上等候启碇了。

Now think well, mother, before you say what I shall bring for you when I come back.

现在,妈妈,好好想一想再告诉我,回来的时候我要带些什么给你。

Mother, do you want heaps and heaps of gold?

妈妈,你要一堆一堆的黄金么?

There, by the banks of golden streams, fields are full of golden harvest.

在金河的两岸,田野里全是金色的稻实。

And in the shade of the forest path the golden champa flowers drop on the ground.

在林荫的路上,金色花也一朵一朵地落在

地上。

I will gather them all for you in many hundred baskets.

我要为你把它们全都收拾起来,放在好几百个篮子里。

Mother, do you want pearls big as the raindrops of autumn?

妈妈,你要秋天的雨点一般大的珍珠么?

I shall cross to the pearl island shore.

我要渡海到珍珠岛的岸上去。

There in the early morning light pearls tremble on the meadow flowers, pearls drop on the grass, and pearls are scattered on the sand in spray by the wild sea-waves.

那个地方,在清晨的曙光里,珠子在草地的野花上颤动,珠子落在绿草上,珠子被汹狂的海浪一大把一大把地撒在沙滩上。

My brother shall have a pair of horses with wings to fly among the clouds.

我的哥哥呢,我要送他一对有翼的马,会在云端飞翔的。

For father I shall bring a magic pen that, without his knowing, will write of itself.

爸爸呢，我要带一支有魔力的笔给他，他还没有觉得，笔就写出字来了。

For you, mother, I must have the casket and jewel that cost seven kings their kingdoms.

你呢，妈妈，我一定要把那个值七个王国的首饰箱和珠宝送给你。

SYMPATHY

同情

If I were only a little puppy, not your baby, mother dear, would you say "No" to me if I tried to eat from your dish?

如果我只是一只小狗,而不是你的小孩,亲爱的妈妈,当我想吃你的盘里的东西时,你要向我说"不"么?

Would you drive me off,saying to me, "Get away, you naughty little puppy?"

你要赶开我,对我说道:"滚开,你这淘气的小狗"么?

Then go, mother, go! I will never come to you when you call me, and never let you feed me any more.

那末,走罢,妈妈,走罢!当你叫唤我的时候,我就永不到你那里去,也永不要你再喂我吃东西了。

If I were only a little green parrot, and not your baby, mother dear, would you keep me chained lest I should fly away?

如果我只是一只绿色的小鹦鹉,而不是你的小孩,亲爱的妈妈,你要把我紧紧地锁住,怕我飞走么?

Would you shake your finger at me and say, "What an ungrateful wretch of a bird! It is gnawing at its chain day and night"?

你要对我摇你的手,说"怎样的一个不知感恩的贱鸟呀!整夜地尽在咬它的链子"么?

Then, go, mother, go! I will run away into the woods; I will never let you take me in your arms again.

那么,走罢,妈妈,走罢!我要跑到树林里去,我就永不再让你抱我在你的臂里了。

VOCATION

职业

When the gong sounds ten in the morning and I walk to school by our lane,

早晨,钟敲十下的时候,我沿着我们的小巷到学校去。

Every day I meet the hawker crying, "Bangles, crystal bangles!"

每天我都遇见那个小贩,他叫道:"镯子呀,亮晶晶的镯子!"

There is nothing to hurry him on, there is no road he must take, no place he must go to, no time when he must come home.

他没有什么事情急着要做,他没有哪条街一定要走,他没有什么地方一定要去,他没有什么时间一定要回家。

I wish I were a hawker, spending my day in the road, crying, "Bangles, crystal bangles!"

我愿意我是一个小贩，在街上过日子，叫着："镯子呀，亮晶晶的镯子！"

When at four in the afternoon I come back from the school,

下午四点，我从学校里回家，

I can see through the gate of that house the gardener digging the ground.

从一家门口,我看得见一个园丁在那里掘地。

He does what he likes with his spade, he soils his clothes with dust, nobody takes him to task if he gets baked in the sun or gets wet.

他用他的锄子,要怎么掘,便怎么掘,他被尘土污了衣裳,如果他被太阳晒黑了或是身上被打湿了,都没有人骂他。

I wish I were a gardener digging away at the garden with nobody to stop me from digging.

我愿意我是一个园丁,在花园里掘地。谁也不来阻止我。

Just as it gets dark in the evening and my mother sends me to bed,

天色刚黑，妈妈就送我上床，

I can see through my open window the watchman walking up and down.

从开着的窗口，我看得见更夫走来走去。

The lane is dark and lonely, and the street-lamp stands like a giant with one red eye in its head.

小巷又黑又冷清，路灯立在那里，像一个头上生着一只红眼睛的巨人。

The watchman swings his lantern and walks with his shadow at his side, and never once goes to bed in his life.

更夫摇着他的提灯，跟他身边的影子一起走着，他一生一次都没有上床去过。

I wish I were a watchman walking the streets all night, chasing the shadows with my lantern.

我愿意我是一个更夫，整夜在街上走，提了灯去追逐影子。

SUPERIOR

长者

Mother, your baby is silly! She is so absurdly childish!

妈妈，你的孩子真傻！她是那么可笑的不懂事！

She does not know the difference between the lights in the streets and the stars.

她不知道路灯和星星的区别。

When we play at eating with pebbles, she thinks they are real food, and tries to put them into her mouth.

当我们玩着把小石子当食物的游戏时，她便以为它们真是吃的东西，竟想放进嘴里去。

When I open a book before her and ask her to learn her a, b, c, she tears the leaves with her hands and roars for joy at nothing; this is your baby's way of doing her lesson.

当我翻开一本书，放在她面前，她在读a、b、c时，却用手把书页撕了，无端快活地叫起来，你的孩子就是这样做功课的。

When I shake my head at her in anger and scold her and call her naughty, she laughs and thinks it great fun.

当我生气地对她摇头，骂她，说她顽皮时，她却哈哈大笑，以为很有趣。

Everybody knows that father is away, but if in play I call aloud "Father", she looks about her in excitement and thinks that father is near.

谁都知道爸爸不在家，但是，如果我在游戏时高声叫一声"爸爸"，她便要高兴地四面张望，以为爸爸真是近在身边。

When I hold my class with the donkeys that our washerman brings to carry away the clothes and I warn her that I am the schoolmaster, she will scream for no reason and call me dada. [elder brother]

当我把洗衣人带来载衣服回去的驴子当作学生,并且警告她说我是老师,她却无缘无故地乱叫起我哥哥来。

Your baby wants to catch the moon.

你的孩子要捉月亮。

She is so funny; she calls Ganesh Ganush.

她是这样的可笑,她把格尼许①唤作琪奴许。

Mother, your baby is silly, she is so absurdly childish!

妈妈,你的孩子真傻,她是那么可笑的不懂事!

【注释】

①格尼许(Ganesh),毁灭之神湿婆的儿子,象头人身。现代印度人也最喜欢用它来做名字的第一个字。

THE LITTLE BIG MAN

小大人

I am small because I am a little child. I shall be big when I am as old as my father is.

我人很小,因为我是一个小孩子,到了我像爸爸一样年纪时,便要变大了。

My teacher will come and say, "It is late, bring your slate and your books."

我的先生要是走来说道:"时候晚了,把你的石板,你的书拿来。"

I shall tell him, "Do you not know I am as big as father? And I must not have lessons any more."

我便要告诉他道:"你不知道我已经同爸爸一样大了么?我决不再学什么功课了。"

My master will wonder and say, "He can leave his books if he likes, for he is grown up."

我的老师便将惊异地说道:"他读书不读书可以随便,因为他是大人了。"

I shall dress myself and walk to the fair where the crowd is thick.

我将自己穿了衣裳,走到人群拥挤的市场里去。

My uncle will come rushing up to me and say, "You will get lost, my boy; let me carry you."

我的叔叔要是跑过来说道:"你要迷路了,我的孩子,让我抱着你吧。"

I shall answer, "Can't you see, uncle, I am as big as father? I must go to the fair alone."

我便要回答道:"你没有看见么,叔叔,我已经同爸爸一样大了?我决定要独自一个人到市场里去。"

Uncle will say, "Yes, he can go wherever he likes, for

he is grown up."

叔叔便将说道:"是的,他随便到哪里去都可以,因为他是大人了。"

Mother will come from her bath when I am giving money to my nurse, for I shall know how to open the box with my key.

当我正拿钱给我保姆时,妈妈便要从浴室中出来,因为我是知道怎样用我的钥匙去开银箱的。

Mother will say, "What are you about, naughty

child?"

妈妈要是说道:"你在做什么呀,顽皮的孩子?"

I shall tell her, "Mother, don't you know, I am as big as father. And I must give silver to my nurse."

我便要告诉她道:"妈妈,你不知道我已经同爸爸一样大了么?我必须拿钱给保姆。"

Mother will say to herself, "He can give money to whom he likes, for he is grown up."

妈妈便将自言自语道:"他可以随便把钱给他所喜欢的人,因为他是大人了。"

In the holiday time in October father will come home and, thinking that I am still a baby, will bring for me from the town little shoes and small silken frocks.

当十月里放假的时候,爸爸将要回家,他会以为我还是一个小孩子,为我从城里带了小鞋子和小绸衫来。

I shall say, "Father, give them to my dada [elder brother], for I am as big as you are."

我便要说道:"爸爸,把这些东西给哥哥吧,因为我已经同你一样大了。"

Father will think and say, "He can buy his own clothes if he likes, for he is grown up."

爸爸便将想了一想,说道;"他可以随便去买他自己穿的衣裳,因为他是大人了。"

TWELVE O'CLOCK

十二点钟

Mother, I do want to leave off my lessons now. I have been at my book all the morning.

妈妈,我真想现在不做功课了。我整个早晨都在念书呢。

You say it is only twelve o'clock. Suppose it isn't any later. Can't you ever think it is afternoon when it is only twelve o'clock?

你说,现在还不过是十二点钟。假定不会晚过十二点吧。难道你不能把不过是十二点钟想象成下午么?

I can easily imagine now that the sun has reached the edge of that rice-field, and the old fisher-woman is gathering herbs for her supper by the side of the pond.

我能够很容易地想象:现在太阳已经到了那片

稻田的边缘上了,老态龙钟的渔婆正在池边采撷香草做她的晚餐。

I can just shut my eyes and think that the shadows are growing darker under the madar tree, and the water in the pond looks shiny black.

我闭上了眼就能够想到,马塔尔树下的阴影是更深黑了,池塘里的水看来黑得发亮。

If twelve o'clock can come in the night, why can't the night come when it is twelve o'clock?

假如十二点钟能够在黑夜里来到,为什么黑夜不能在十二点钟的时候来到呢?

The Crescent Moon

AUTHORSHIP
著作家

You say that father writes a lot of books, but what he writes I don't understand.

你说爸爸写了许多书,而我却不懂得他所写的东西。

He was reading to you all the evening, but could you really make out what he meant?

他整个黄昏读书给你听,但是你真懂得他的意思么?

What nice stories, mother, you can tell us! Why can't father write like that, I wonder?

妈妈,你给我们讲的故事,真是好听呀!我很奇怪,爸爸为什么不能写那样的书呢?

Did he never hear from his own mother stories of giants and fairies and princesses?

难道他从来没有从他自己的妈妈那里听见过巨人和神仙、公主的故事么?

Has he forgotten them all?
还是已经完全忘记了?

Often when he gets late for his bath you have to go and call him an hundred times.
他常常耽误了沐浴,你不得不走去叫他一百多次。

You wait and keep his dishes warm for him, but he goes on writing and forgets.
你总要等候着,把他的菜温着等他,但他忘了,还尽管写下去。

Father always plays at making books.
爸爸老是以著书为游戏。

If ever I go to play in father's room, you come and call me, "what a naughty child!"

如果我一走进爸爸房里去游戏,你就要走来叫道:"真是一个顽皮的孩子!"

If I make the slightest noise, you say, "Don't you see that father's at his work?"

如果我稍微出一点声音,你就要说:"你没有看见你爸爸正在工作么?"

What's the fun of always writing and writing?

老是写了又写,有什么趣味呢?

When I take up father's pen or pencil and write upon his book just as he does——a, b, c, d, e, f, g, h, i, —— why do you get cross with me, then, mother?

当我拿起爸爸的钢笔或铅笔,像他一模一样地在他的书上写着——a、b、c、d、e、f、g、h、i——那时,你为什么跟我生气呢,妈妈?

You never say a word when father writes.

爸爸写时,你却从来不说一句话。

When my father wastes such heaps of paper, mother, you don't seem to mind at all.

当我爸爸耗费了那么一大堆纸时,妈妈,你似乎全不在乎。

But if I take only one sheet to make a boat with, you say, "Child, how troublesome you are!"

但是，如果我只取了一张纸去做一只船，你却要说："孩子，你真讨厌！"

What do you think of father's spoiling sheets and sheets of paper with black marks all over on both sides?

你对于爸爸拿黑点子涂满了纸的两面，污损了许多许多张纸，你心里以为怎样呢？

THE WICKED POSTMAN

恶邮差

Why do you sit there on the floor so quiet and silent, tell me, mother dear?

你为什么坐在那边地板上不言不动的,告诉我呀,亲爱的妈妈?

The rain is coming in through the open window, making you all wet, and you don't mind it.

雨从开着的窗口打进来了,把你身上全打湿了,你却不管。

Do you hear the gong striking four? It is time for my brother to come home from school.

你听见钟已打四下了么?正是哥哥从学校里回家的时候了。

What has happened to you that you look so strange?

到底发生了什么事,你的神色这样不对?

Haven't you got a letter from father today?

你今天没有接到爸爸的信么?

I saw the postman bringing letters in his bag for almost everybody in the town.

我看见邮差在他的袋里带了许多信来,几乎镇里的每个人都分送到了。

Only, father's letters he keeps to read himself. I am sure the postman is a wicked man.

只有爸爸的信,他留起来给他自己看。我确信这个邮差是个坏人。

But don't be unhappy about that, mother dear.

但是不要因此不乐呀,亲爱的妈妈。

Tomorrow is market day in the next village. You ask your maid to buy some pens and papers.

明天是邻村市集的日子。你叫女仆去买些笔和纸来。

I myself will write all father's letters, you will not find a single mistake.

我自己会写爸爸所写的一切信,使你找不出一点错处来。

I shall write from A right up to K.

我要从A字一直写到K字。

But, mother, why do you smile?

但是,妈妈,你为什么笑呢?

You don't believe that I can write as nicely as father does!

你不相信我能写得同爸爸一样好?

But I shall rule my paper carefully, and write all the letters beautifully big.

但是我将用心画格子，把所有的字母都写得又大又美。

When I finish my writing, do you think I shall be so foolish as father and drop it into the horrid postman's bag?

当我写好了时，你以为我也像爸爸那样傻，把它投入可怕的邮差的袋中么？

I shall bring it to you myself without waiting, and letter by letter help you to read my writing.

我立刻就自己送来给你，而且一个字母，一个字母地帮助你读。

I know the postman does not like to give you the really nice letters.

我知道那邮差是不肯把真正的好信送给你的。

THE HERO

英雄

Mother, let us imagine we are travelling, and passing through a strange and dangerous country.

妈妈,让我们想象我们正在旅行,经过一个陌生而危险的国土。

You are riding in a palanquin and I am trotting by you on a red horse.

你坐在一顶轿子里,我骑着一匹红马,在你旁边跑着。

It is evening and the sun goes down. The waste of Joradighi lies wan and grey before us. The land is desolate and barren.

是黄昏的时候,太阳已经下山了。约拉地希的荒地疲乏而灰暗地展开在我们面前。大地是凄凉而荒芜的。

You are frightened and thinking——"I know not where we have come to."

你害怕了,想道——"我不知道我们到了什么地方了。"

I say to you, "Mother, do not be afraid."
我对你说道:"妈妈,不要害怕。"

The meadow is prickly with spiky grass, and through it runs a narrow broken path.

草地上刺蓬蓬地长着针尖似的草,一条狭而崎岖的小道通过这块草地。

There are no cattle to be seen in the wide field, they have gone to their village stalls.

在这片广大的地面上看不见一只牛,它们已经回到它们村里的牛棚去了。

It grows dark and dim on the land and sky, and we

cannot tell where we are going.

天色黑了下来，大地和天空都显得朦朦胧胧的，而我们不能说出我们正走向什么所在。

Suddenly you call me and ask me in a whisper, "What light is that near the bank？"

突然间，你叫我，悄悄地问我道："靠近河岸的是什么火光呀？"

Just then there bursts out a fearful yell, and figures come running towards us.

正在那个时候，一阵可怕的呐喊声爆发了，好些人影子向我们跑过来。

You sit crouched in your palanquin and repeat the names of the gods in prayer.

你蹲坐在你的轿子里，嘴里反复地祷念着神的名字。

The bearers, shaking in terror, hide themselves in the

thorny bush.

轿夫们,怕得发抖,躲藏在荆棘丛中。

I shout to you, "Don't be afraid, mother. I am here."

我向你喊道:"不要害怕,妈妈,有我在这里。"

With long sticks in their hands and hair all wild about their heads, they come nearer and nearer.

他们手里执着长棒,头发披散着,越走越近了。

I shout, "Have a care! you villains! One step more and you are dead men."

我喊道:"要当心!你们这些坏蛋!再向前走一步,你们就要送命了。"

They give another terrible yell and rush forward.

他们又发出一阵可怕的呐喊声,向前冲过来。

You clutch my hand and say, "Dear boy, for heaven's sake, keep away from them."

你抓住我的手,说道:"好孩子,看在上天的面子上,躲开他们吧。"

I say, "Mother, just you watch me."

我说道:"妈妈,你瞧我的。"

Then I spur my horse for a wild gallop, and my sword and buckler clash against each other.

于是我刺策着我的马匹,猛奔过去,我的剑和盾彼此碰着作响。

The fight becomes so fearful, mother, that it would give you a cold shudder could you see it from your palanquin.

这一场战斗是那么激烈,妈妈,如果你从轿子里看得见的话,你一定会发冷颤的。

Many of them fly, and a great number are cut

to pieces.

他们之中，许多人逃走了，还有好些人被砍杀了。

I know you are thinking, sitting all by yourself, that your boy must be dead by this time.

我知道你那时独自坐在那里，心里正在想着，你的孩子这时候一定已经死了。

But I come to you all stained with blood, and say, "Mother, the fight is over now."

但是我跑到你的跟前，浑身溅满了鲜血，说道："妈妈，现在战争已经结束了。"

You come out and kiss me, pressing me to your heart, and you say to yourself,

你从轿子里走出来，吻着我，把我搂在你的心头，你自言自语地说道：

"I don't know what I should do if I hadn't my boy to escort me."

"如果我没有我的孩子护送我,我简直不知道怎么办才好。"

A thousand useless things happen day after day, and why couldn't such a thing come true by chance?

一千件无聊的事天天在发生,为什么这样一件事不能够偶然实现呢?

It would be like a story in a book.

这很像一本书里的一个故事。

My brother would say, "Is it possible? I always thought he was so delicate!"

我的哥哥要说道:"这是可能的事么?我老是在想,他是那么嫩弱呢!"

Our village people would all say in amazement, "Was

it not lucky that the boy was with his mother?"

我们村里的人们都要惊讶地说道:"这孩子正和他妈妈在一起,这不是很幸运么?"

THE END
告别

It is time for me to go, mother; I am going.

是我走的时候了,妈妈,我走了。

When in the paling darkness of the lonely dawn you stretch out your arms for your baby in the bed, I shall say, "Baby is not there!"——mother, I am going.

当清寂的黎明,你在暗中伸出双臂,要抱你睡在床上的孩子时,我要说道:"孩子不在那里呀!"——妈妈,我走了。

I shall become a delicate draught of air and caress you, and I shall be ripples in the water when you bathe, and kiss you and kiss you again.

我要变成一股清风抚摸着你,我要变成水的涟漪,当你浴时,把你吻了又吻。

In the gusty night when the rain patters on the leaves you will hear my whisper in your bed, and my laughter will flash with the lightning through the open window into your room.

大风之夜，当雨点在树叶中淅沥时，你在床上，会听见我的微语，当电光从开着的窗口闪进你的屋里时，我的笑声也偕了它一同闪进了。

If you lie awake, thinking of your baby till late into the night. I shall sing to you from the stars, "Sleep mother, sleep."

如果你醒着躺在床上，想你的孩子到深夜，我便要从星空向你唱道："睡呀妈妈，睡呀。"

On the straying moonbeams I shall steal over your bed, and lie upon your bosom while you sleep.

我要坐在各处游荡的月光上，偷偷地来到你的床上，乘你睡着时，躺在你的胸上。

I shall become a dream, and through the little opening of your eyelids I shall slip into the depths of your sleep; and when you wake up and look round startled, like a twinkling firefly I shall flit out into the darkness.

我要变成一个梦儿,从你的眼皮的微缝中,钻到你睡眠的深处。当你醒来吃惊地四望时,我便如闪耀的萤火似的熠熠地向暗中飞去了。

When, on the great festival of Puja, the neighbours' children come and play about the house, I shall melt into the music of the flute and throb in your heart all day.

当普耶节日①,邻舍家的孩子们来屋里游玩时,我便要融化在笛声里,整日在你心头震荡。

Dear auntie will come with Puja-presents and will ask, "Where is our baby, sister?Mother, you will tell her softly, "He is in the pupils of my eyes, he is in my body and in my soul."

亲爱的阿姨带了普耶礼②来,问道:"我们的孩子在哪里,姊姊?"妈妈。你将要柔声地告诉她:"他现在是在我的瞳仁里,他现在是在我的身体里,在我的灵魂里。"

【注释】

①普耶(Puja),意为"祭神大典",这里的"普耶节",是指印度十月间的"难近母祭日"。

②普耶礼,指这个节日亲友相互馈送的礼物。

THE RECALL

召唤

The night was dark when she went away, and they slept.

她走的时候,夜间黑漆漆的,他们都睡了。

The night is dark now, and I call for her, "Come back, my darling; the world is asleep; and no one would know, if you came for a moment while stars are gazing at stars."

现在,夜间也是黑漆漆的,我唤她道:"回来,我的宝贝;世界都在沉睡;当星星互相凝视的时候,你来一会儿是没有人会知道的。"

She went away when the trees were in bud and the spring was young.

她走的时候,树木正在萌芽,春光刚刚来到。

Now the flowers are in high bloom and I call, "Come back, my darling. The children gather and scatter flowers in reckless sport. And if you come and take one little blossom no one will miss it."

现在花已盛开,我唤道:"回来,我的宝贝。孩子们漫不经心地在游戏,把花聚在一起,又把它们散开。你如走来,拿一朵小花去,没有

The Crescent Moon

人会发觉的。"

Those that used to play are playing still, so spendthrift is life.

常常在游戏的那些人,仍然还在那里游戏,生命总是如此浪费。

I listen to their chatter and call, "Come back, my darling, for mother's heart is full to the brim with love, and if you come to snatch only one little kiss from her no one will grudge it."

我静听他们的空谈,便唤道:"回来,我的宝贝,妈妈的心里充满着爱,你如走来,仅仅从她那里接一个小小的吻,没有人会妒忌的。"

THE FIRST JASMINES

第一次的茉莉

Ah, these jasmines, these white jasmines!

呵,这些茉莉花,这些白的茉莉花!

I seem to remember the first day when I filled my hands with these jasmines, these white jasmines.

我仿佛记得我第一次双手满捧着这些茉莉花,这些白的茉莉花的时候。

I have loved the sunlight, the sky and the green earth;

我喜爱那日光,那天空,那绿色的大地;

I have heard the liquid murmur of the river through the darkness of midnight;

我听见那河水淙淙的流声,在黑漆的午夜里传过来;

Autumn sunsets have come to me at the bend of a road in the lonely waste, like a bride raising her veil to accept her lover.

秋天的夕阳，在荒原上大路转角处迎我，如新妇揭起她的面纱迎接她的爱人。

Yet my memory is still sweet with the first white jasmines that I held in my hand when I was a child.

但我想起孩提时第一次捧在手里的白茉莉，

心里充满着甜蜜的回忆。

Many a glad day has come in my life, and I have laughed with merrymakers on festival nights.

我生平有过许多快活的日子,在节日宴会的晚上,我曾跟着说笑话的人大笑。

On grey mornings of rain I have crooned many an idle song.

在灰暗的雨天的早晨,我吟哦过许多飘逸的诗篇。

The Crescent Moon

I have worn round my neck the evening wreath of bakulas woven by the hand of love.

我颈上戴过爱人手织的醉花的花圈，作为晚装。

Yet my heart is sweet with the memory of the first fresh jasmines that filled my hands when I was a child.

但我想起孩提时第一次捧在手里的白茉莉，心里充满着甜蜜的回忆。

THE BANYAN TREE

榕树

O you shaggy-headed banyan tree standing on the bank of the pond, have you forgotten the little child, like the birds that have nested in your branches and left you?

喂,你站在池边的蓬头的榕树,你可会忘记了那小小的孩子,就像那在你的枝上筑巢又离开了你的鸟儿似的孩子?

Do you not remember how he sat at the window and wondered at the tangle of your roots that plunged underground?

你不记得是他怎样坐在窗内,诧异地望着你深入地下的纠缠的树根么?

The women would come to fill their jars in the pond, and your huge black shadow would wriggle on the water like sleep struggling to wake up.

妇人们常到池边，汲了满罐的水去，你的大黑影便在水面上摇动，好像睡着的人挣扎着要醒来似的。

Sunlight danced on the ripples like restless tiny shuttles weaving golden tapestry.

日光在微波上跳舞，好像不停不息的小梭在织着金色的花毡。

Two ducks swam by the weedy margin above their shadows, and the child would sit still and think.

两只鸭子挨着芦苇,在芦苇影子上游来游去,孩子静静地坐在那里想着。

He longed to be the wind and blow through your rustling branches, to be your shadow and lengthen with the day on the water, to be a bird and perch on your top-most twig, and to float like those ducks among the weeds and shadows.

他想做风,吹过你的萧萧的枝杈;想做你的影子,在水面上,随了日光而俱长;想做一只鸟儿,栖息在你的最高枝上;还想做那两只鸭,在芦苇与阴影中间游来游去。

The Crescent Moon

BENEDICTION

祝福

Bless this little heart. this white soul that has won the kiss of heaven for our earth.

祝福这个小心灵，这个洁白的灵魂，他为我们的大地，赢得了天的接吻。

He loves the light of the sun, he loves the sight of his mother's face.

他爱日光，他爱见他妈妈的脸。

He has not learned to despise the dust, and to hanker after gold.

他没有学会厌恶尘土而渴求黄金。

Clasp him to your heart and bless him.

紧抱他在你的心里，并且祝福他。

He has come into this land of an hundred cross-roads.

他已来到这个歧路百出的大地上了。

I know not how he chose you from the crowd, came to your door, and grasped your hand to ask his way.

我不知道他怎么从群众中选出你来,来到你的门前抓住你的手问路。

He will follow you, laughing and talking, and not a doubt in his heart.

他笑着,谈着,跟着你走,心里没有一点儿疑惑。

Keep his trust, lead him straight and bless him.

不要辜负他的信任,引导他到正路,并且祝福他。

Lay your hand on his head, and pray that though the waves underneath grow threatening, yet the breath from above may come and fill his sails and waft him to the haven of peace.

把你的手按在他的头上,祈求着:底下的波涛虽然险恶，然而从上面来的风，会鼓起他的船帆，送他到和平的港口的。

Forget him not in your hurry, let him come to your heart and bless him.

不要在忙碌中把他忘了，让他来到你的心里，并且祝福他。

THE GIFT

赠品

I want to give you something, my child, for we are drifting in the stream of the world.

我要送些东西给你,我的孩子,因为我们同是漂泊在世界的溪流中的。

Our lives will be carried apart, and our love forgotten.

我们的生命将被分开,我们的爱也将被忘记。

But I am not so foolish as to hope that I could buy your heart with my gifts.

但我没有那样傻,希望能用我的赠品来买你的心。

Young is your life, your path long, and you drink the love we bring you at one draught and turn and run away from us.

你的生命正是青青,你的道路也长着呢,你一口气饮尽了我们带给你的爱，便回身离开我们跑了。

You have your play and your playmates. What harm is there if you have no time or thought for us.

你有你的游戏，有你的游伴。如果你没有时间同我们在一起，如果你想不到我们，那有什么害处呢？

We, indeed, have leisure enough in old age to count the days that are past, to cherish in our hearts what our hands have lost for ever.

我们呢,自然的,在老年时,会有许多闲暇的时间中,去计算那过去的日子,把我们手里永久失了的东西,在心里爱抚着。

The river runs swift with a song, breaking through all barriers. But the mountain stays and remembers, and follows her with his love.

河流唱着歌很快地流去,冲破所有的堤防。但是山峰留在那里,忆念着,满怀依依之情。

MY SONG

我的歌

This song of mine will wind its music around you, my child, like the fond arms of love.

我的孩子，我这一支歌将扬起它的乐声围绕你的身旁，好像那爱情的热恋的手臂一样。

This song of mine will touch your forehead like a kiss of blessing.

我这一只歌将触着你的前额,好像那祝福的接吻一样。

When you are alone it will sit by your side and whisper in your ear, when you are in the crowd it will fence you about with aloofness.

当你只是一个人的时候,它将坐在你的身旁,在你耳边微语着;当你在人群中的时候,它将围住你,使你超然物外。

My song will be like a pair of wings to your dreams, it will transport your heart to the verge of the unknown.

我的歌将成为你的梦的翼翅,它将把你的心移送到不可知的岸边。

It will be like the faithful star overhead when dark night is over your road.

当黑夜覆盖在你路上的时候,它又将成为那照临在你头上的忠实的星光。

The Crescent Moon

My song will sit in the pupils of your eyes, and will carry your sight into the heart of things.

我的歌又将坐在你眼睛的瞳仁里，将你的视线带入万物的心里。

And when my voice is silent in death, my song will speak in your living heart.

当我的声音因死亡而沉寂时，我的歌仍将在我活泼泼的心中唱着。

微信扫码
拓展视频　图文资讯
趣味测评　阅读分享

THE CHILD-ANGEL

孩子天使

They clamour and fight, they doubt and despair, they know no end to their wranglings.

他们喧哗争斗,他们怀疑失望,他们辩论而没有结果。

Let your life come amongst them like a flame of light, my child, unflickering and pure, and delight them into silence.

我的孩子,让你的生命到他们当中去,如一线镇定而纯洁之光,使他们愉悦而沉默。

They are cruel in their greed and their envy, their words are like hidden knives thirsting for blood.

他们的贪心和妒忌是残忍的;他们的话,好像暗藏的刀,渴欲饮血。

Go and stand amidst their scowling hearts, my child, and let your gentle eyes fall upon them like the forgiving peace of the evening over the strife of the day.

我的孩子，去，去站在他们愤懑的心中，把你的和善的眼光落在它们上面，好像那傍晚的宽宏大量的和平，覆盖着日间的骚扰一样。

Let them see your face, my child, and thus know the

meaning of all things; let them love you and thus love each other.

我的孩子，让他们望着你的脸，因此能够知道一切事物的意义；让他们爱你，因此他们能够相爱。

Come and take your seat in the bosom of the limitless, my child. At sunrise open and raise your heart like a blossoming flower, and at sunset bend your head and in silence complete the worship of the day.

来，坐在无垠的胸膛上，我的孩子。朝阳出来时，开放而且抬起你的心，像一朵盛开的花；夕阳落下时，低下你的头，默默地做完这一天的礼拜。

The Crescent Moon

THE LAST BARGAIN

最后的买卖

"Come and hire me," I cried, while in the morning I was walking on the stone-paved road.

早晨，我在石铺的路上走时，我叫道："来雇用我呀。"

Sword in hand, the King came in his chariot.

皇帝坐着马车，手里拿着剑走来。

He held my hand and said, "I will hire you with my power."

他拉着我的手，说道："我要用权力来雇用你。"

But his power counted for nought, and he went away in his chariot.

但是他的权力算不了什么，他坐着马车走了。

In the heat of the midday the houses stood with shut doors.

正午炎热的时候,家家户户的门都闭着。

I wandered along the crooked lane.

我沿着屈曲的小巷走去。

An old man came out with his bag of gold.

一个老人带着一袋金钱走出来。

He pondered and said, "I will hire you with my money."

他斟酌了一下,说道:"我要用金钱来雇用你。"

He weighed his coins one by one, but I turned away.

他一个一个地数着他的钱,而我却转身离去了。

It was evening. The garden hedge was all flower.

黄昏了,花园的篱上满开着花。

The fairy maid came out and said, "I will hire you with a smile."

美人走出来,说道:"我要用微笑来雇用你。"

Her smile paled and melted into tears, and she went back alone into the dark.

她的微笑黯淡了,化成泪容了,她孤寂地回身走进黑暗里去。

The sun glistened on the sand, and the sea waves broke waywardly.

太阳照耀在沙地上,海波任性地浪花四溅。

A child sat playing with shells.

一个小孩坐在那里玩贝壳。

He raised his head and seemed to know me, and said, "I hire you with nothing."

他抬起头来，好像认识我似的，说道："我雇你不用什么东西。"

From thenceforward that bargain struck in child's play made me a free man.

在这个小孩的游戏中做成的买卖，使我从此以后成了一个自由的人。

图文资讯 拓展书籍内容,开阔阅读视野。

拓展视频 观看在线视频,激发阅读兴趣。

趣味测评 测评阅读习惯,获取阅读建议。

阅读分享 分享阅读心得,碰撞思维火花。

扫码进入 线上阅读空间

ONLINE READING SPACE

让知识照耀人生